T0198990

Eleanor

the Snooty Pigeon

Amanda Sue

Print information available on the last page.

Rev. date: 01/04/2017

To order additional copies of this book, contact:
Xlibris
1-888-795-4274
www.Xlibris.com
Orders@Xlibris.com

Eleanor

the Snooty Pigeon

One day, while at the feeder, a tiny finch was eating peacefully and enjoying a wonderful morning. That was until Eleanor, the very loud and very snooty pigeon, arrived.

Eleanor was very outspoken and began to say mean things, such as, "This isn't really the proper place for a bird, such as you, to be eating. Why don't you find a place with more of your kind there?"

The finch became very sad and decided she should go and flew away. Eleanor was very pleased that she had her favorite spot all to herself again. You see, Eleanor felt that there wasn't another bird that was as great a bird as she.

Day after day, Eleanor took pride in pushing away and bullying other smaller birds. She was mean and rude and would never even give them the time a day as to even ask them their names.

One day, while at her favorite bird feeder, she noticed a shiny object on the ground. Eleanor quickly flew down to see what it was. But Eleanor didn't notice the danger she was about to fly into. She was so curious to see what it was that she just went for it, never thinking she could get hurt or into trouble.

As she got closer to it, she could see a clear glass like look just before the object. Eleanor was moving so fast and was so sure of herself she flew right into it. It was then that this snooty, loud, and somewhat mean pigeon Eleanor had realized she was in a very bad way.

For when she flew in so quickly, she didn't notice she was flying into the plastic rings from a pack of soda. This pack of rings was someone's garbage that had been left on the ground. This was very bad, and Eleanor was stuck. She wiggled and struggled but could not move at all. The more she moved, the more stuck she became, and finally, she was exhausted and laid down.

Just then, the little finch from days before flew over and noticed that Eleanor was in trouble. The kind little finch knew that this pigeon was mean and did not deserve her help at all. But this very kind finch could not find it in her heart to just leave her alone.

The finch flew down and immediately took action to get Eleanor out of this terrible situation. The finch was very small, but she worked with the strength of a much larger bird; her heart was pure, and she tried with all her might.

Finally, she was able to free poor Eleanor from the plastic she was trapped in. They then flew up to the nearest tree where it was safe. It was there that Eleanor realized just how horrible she had been to all those other birds.

Eleanor was so ashamed of her behavior, and she began to thank this amazing little finch for her selfless actions and kind heart. Eleanor knew she also had to apologize for all the mean things she had done and said before. But this was not the only bird she had treated very rudely.

So she decided to apologize to all the birds she had treated wrongly and been rude to, and from then on, she never mistreated another bird ever again. Eleanor had realized that she was not the most important bird there ever was and that the way you treat others matters.

And so this is the end of the story of Eleanor the snooty pigeon!

Printed in the United States
By Bookmasters